Spots

Written by Carol Krueger

jaguar

Look at all the spots
on these animals.
The spots look different,
but they all help the animals
in different ways.

dog

deer

butterfly

3

Spots help this leopard hide
when it is looking for food.
It can hide in the long grass
so other animals won't see it.
Then the leopard can
jump out at them.

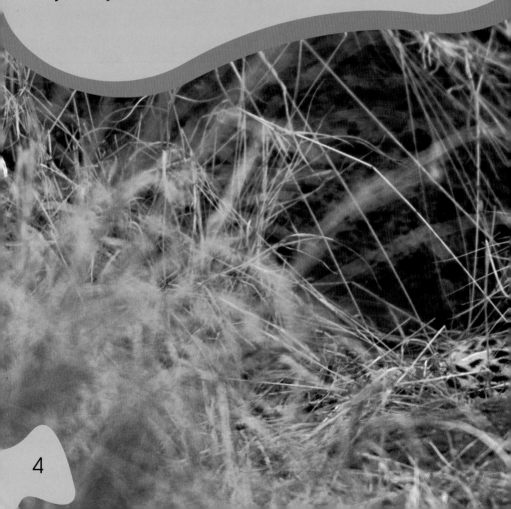

Spots can help animals
hide from danger.
This baby deer has spots
that help it hide.
When the baby gets bigger,
the spots will go away.

This bird has its eggs
on the beach.
The eggs have spots
on them.
The spots keep
the eggs safe.
They make the eggs
look like stones.

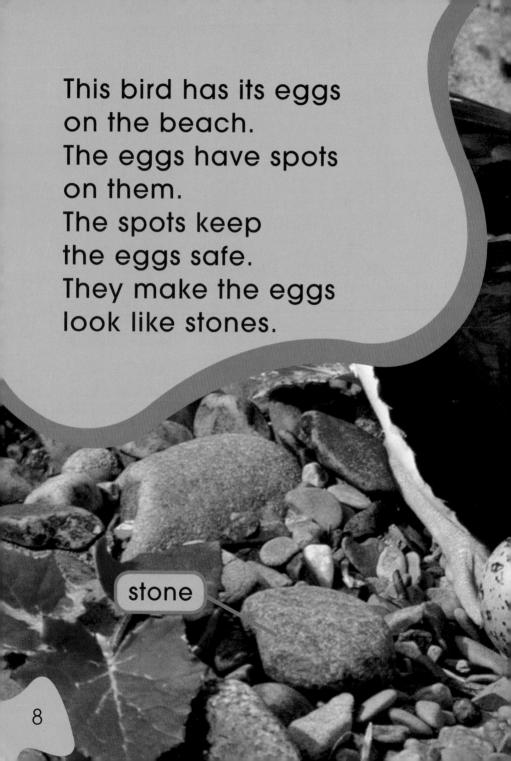

stone

eggs

red spot

Some spots tell other animals
to stay away.
This spider has a red spot
on its back.
It tells other animals that
the spider is dangerous.

This butterfly has
two big spots on its wings.
The spots look
like big eyes.
They help other butterflies
see it.

Animals can have spots
that make them
look different.
The spots on this dog
are not like the spots
on other dogs.

Big cats have different spots, too.

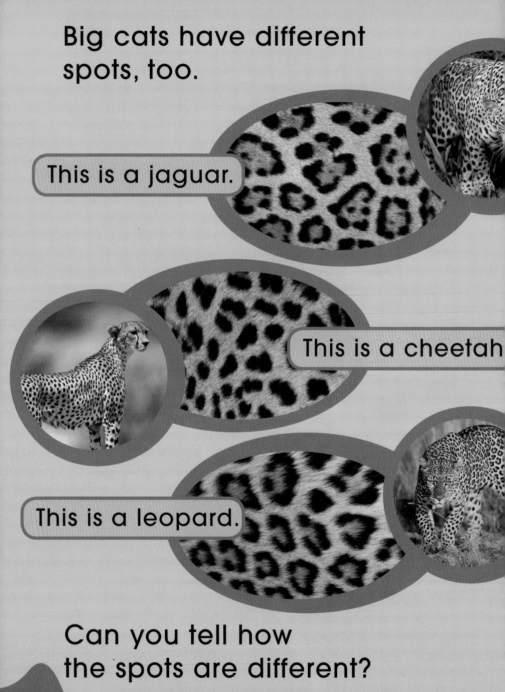

This is a jaguar.

This is a cheetah

This is a leopard.

Can you tell how the spots are different?

14

Index

Guide Notes

Title: Spots
Stage: Early (4) – Green

Genre: Nonfiction
Approach: Guided Reading
Processes: Thinking Critically, Exploring Language, Processing Information
Written and Visual Focus: Photographs (static images), Labels, Captions, Index
Word Count: 189

THINKING CRITICALLY
(sample questions)
- Look at the front cover and the title. Ask the children what they know about animals that have spots.
- Read the title to the children.
- Focus the children's attention on the index. Ask: "What are you going to find out about in this book?"
- If you want to find out about a baby deer's spots, what page would you look on?
- If you want to find out about a butterfly with spots on its wings, what page would you look on?
- Look at pages 6 and 7. Why do you think the baby deer's spots go away when it gets bigger?
- Look at page 14. Why do you think the big cats have different spots?

EXPLORING LANGUAGE

Terminology
Title, cover, photographs, author, photographers

Vocabulary
Interest words: leopard, deer, spider, butterfly, jaguar, cheetah
High-frequency words: won't, tell, keep
Positional words: on, out, in
Compound word: butterfly

Print Conventions
Capital letter for sentence beginnings, periods, commas, question mark